WILLOUGHBY
& THE MOON

R0055132302

W9-BAI-539

E FOLEY
Foley, Greg E.,
Willoughby & the moon /

PALM BEACH COUNTY
LIBRARY SYSTEM
3650 Summit Boulevard
West Palm Beach, FL 33406-4198

Balzer + Bray
An Imprint of HarperCollins*Publishers*

Balzer & Bray is an imprint of HarperCollins Publishers.

Willoughby & the Moon
Copyright © 2010 by Greg Foley
All rights reserved. Manufactured in China.
No part of this book may be used or reproduced in any manner whatsoever without
written permission except in the case of brief quotations embodied in critical articles
and reviews. For information address HarperCollins Children's Books, a division of
HarperCollins Publishers, 10 East 53rd Street, New York, NY 10022.
www.harpercollinschildrens.com

Library of Congress Cataloging-in-Publication Data
Foley, Greg E.
    Willoughby & the moon / by Greg Foley. — 1st ed.
        p.   cm.
    Summary: When Willoughby Smith discovers a snail sitting atop the moon in his
closet one night, the two help each other overcome their fears.
    ISBN 978-0-06-154753-9 (trade bdg.) — ISBN 978-0-06-154754-6 (lib. bdg.)
    [1. Moon—Fiction.   2. Fear—Fiction.   3. Snails—Fiction.]   I. Title.   II. Title:
Willoughby and the moon.
PZ7.F35Wi   2010   2009020528
[E]—dc22   CIP
                                                                      AC

10 11 12 13 14   LEO   10 9 8 7 6 5 4 3 2 1
❖
First Edition

WILLOUGHBY
& THE MOON
BY
GREG FOLEY

Willoughby Smith could not sleep. Every night, the moon outside his window got a little smaller. Until one night it wasn't there at all, and his bedroom became very dark.

"Are you afraid?" his mother asked.

"No!" Willoughby said. "I just wonder where the moon is."

Later, Willoughby saw a soft light coming from his closet. He looked inside and found the strangest thing. There was the moon, and on it stood a giant snail.

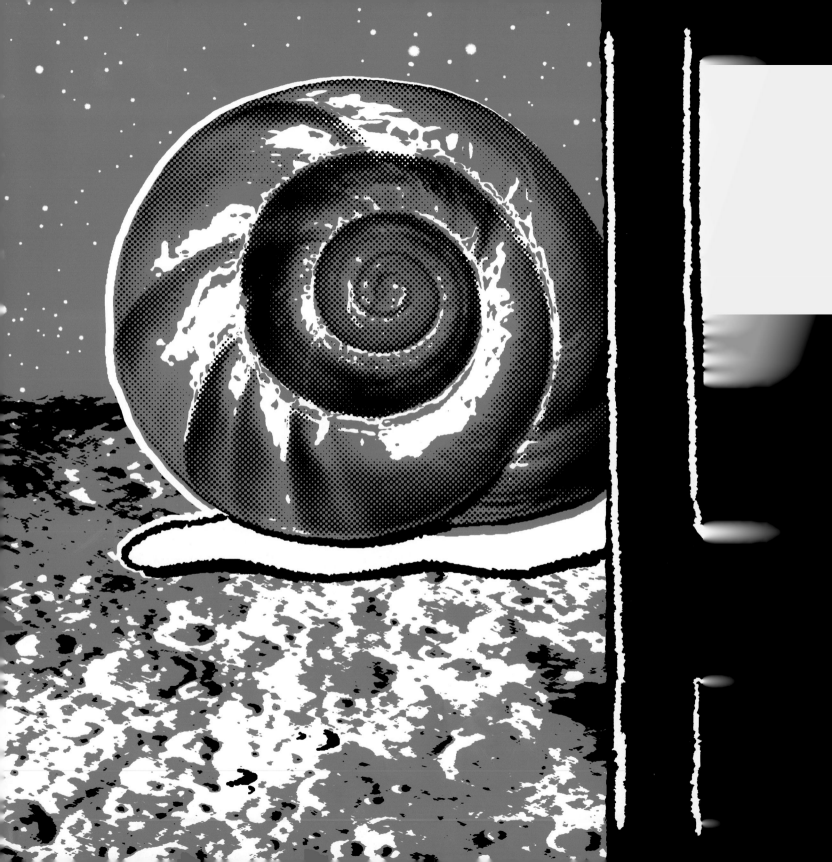

Willoughby tapped on the shell. "Excuse me," he said. "What are you doing in my closet?"

Two eyes peeked out. "I lost my favorite silver ball," said the snail. "And the moon is so big, I'll probably never find it."

Willoughby puffed up his chest. "I'll bet I can find it," he said. "Maybe it's behind those rocks."

"I don't know," said the snail. "Those rocks look scary."

"Rocks are nothing to be scared of,"
Willoughby said. And he checked all around
them, but there was no sign of the ball.
"I told you," said the snail.
Then Willoughby spotted something round.

It was a dusty old moon buggy.

"Let's take a ride and look inside these craters," Willoughby said.

"Not me," said the snail. "That sounds bumpy."

"A bumpy ride is nothing to worry about," Willoughby said. He rode the buggy all around the craters while the snail watched.

Still, no luck . . .

. . . until Willoughby spied something shiny.
"I think I see it!" he called to the snail.

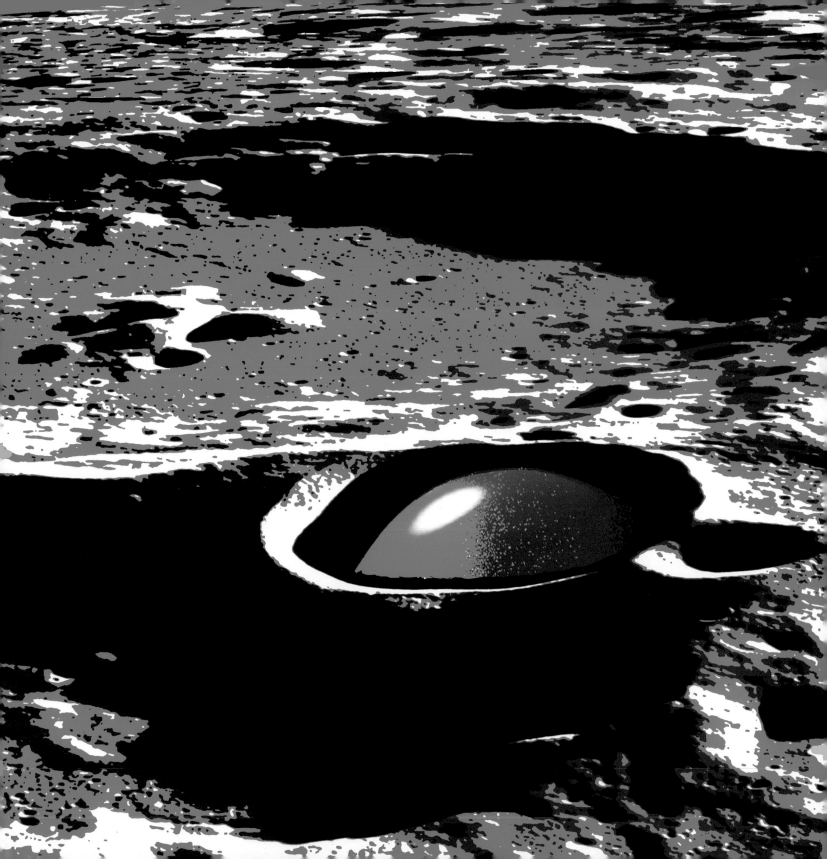

This time, they found an empty space pod.

"We've only checked one half of the moon," Willoughby said. "Why don't we rocket to the other side?"

"Oh no," said the snail. "I'm afraid of heights."

"Heights are no big deal," Willoughby said.

So Willoughby flew the space pod to the far side of the moon. He looked out at all the rocks, craters, and mountaintops. The ball was nowhere in sight.

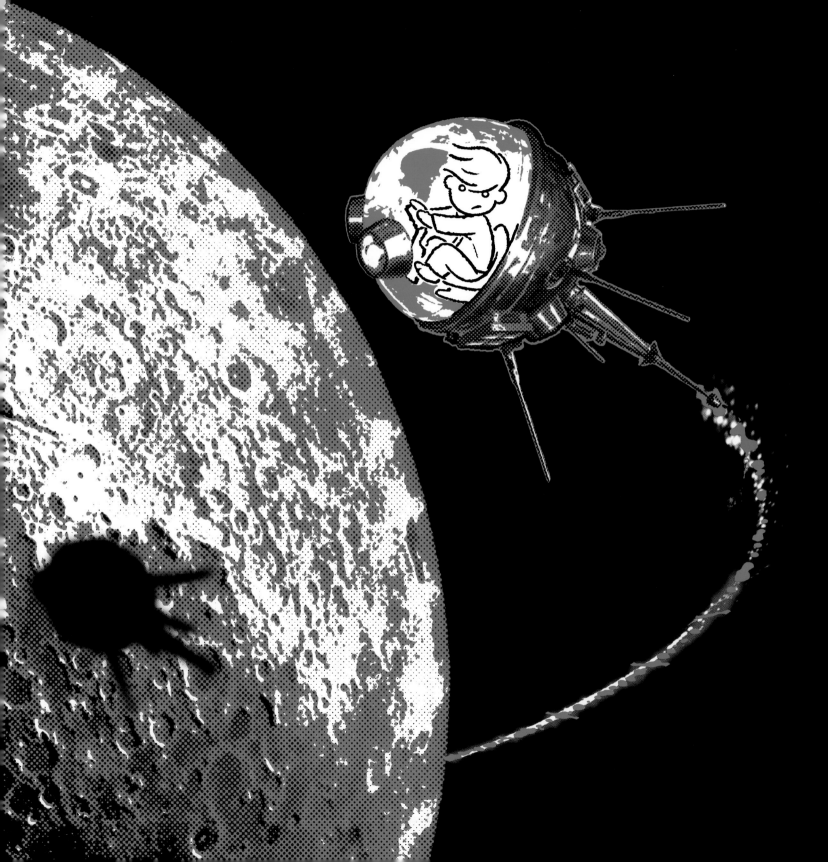

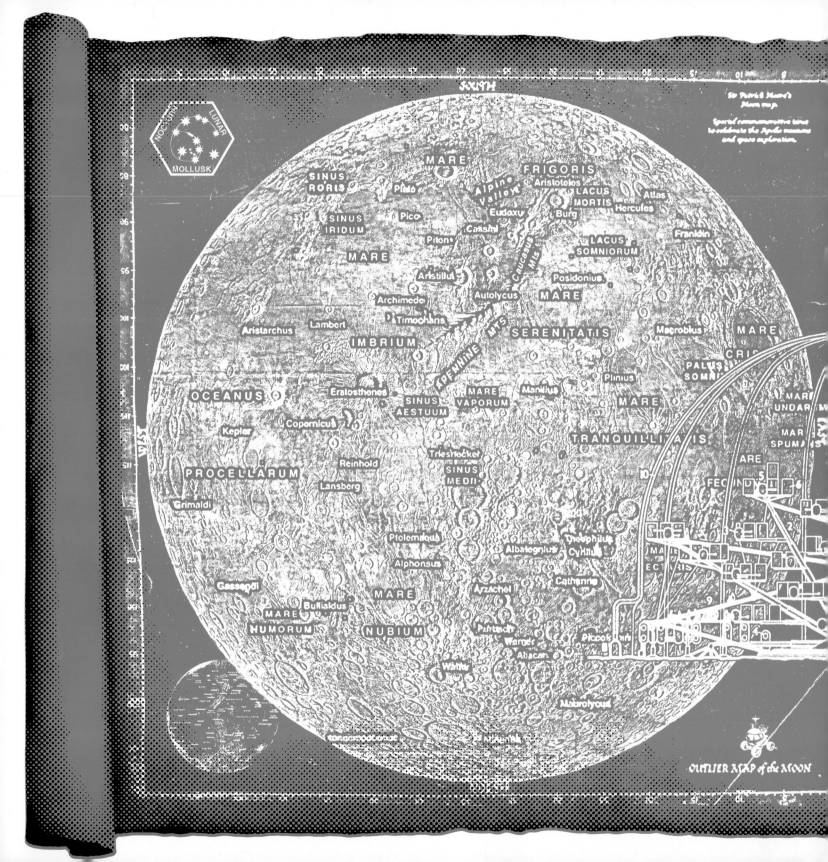

MOONCORE

LUNAR CAVERN SYSTEM
SUB TERRA

SELF-GROWING LUNAR FACTORY

EARTH AND MOON COMPARED

Earth   Moon

When Willoughby got back, the snail told him, "There's only one place left to look." And he unrolled a map showing the inside of the moon.

Willoughby followed the snail to the mouth of a huge cave. Then he stopped. "I can't go in there," he said. "It's too dark."

"The dark is nothing to be afraid of," said the snail. "Look! I'll show you."

So Willoughby sat and watched as the snail disappeared into the cave.

He waited and waited. But after a while, there was no sign of the snail. "Where could he be?" Willoughby wondered. The cave was very dark. But Willoughby was worried about the snail.

So he decided to do something very brave. Inch by inch, Willoughby crept into the dark. "I hope the snail is okay."

When he could no longer see the entrance, Willoughby almost turned back. But then he saw something round and shiny and familiar.

Up ahead was a bright cavern. Everywhere Willoughby looked in that cavern were giant snails. And there was his friend, holding a silver ball high in the air.

"Look what I found!" the snail shouted.

Outside, Willoughby and the snails played all kinds of games. In some, it was the snails versus Willoughby, and in others, it was Willoughby versus the snails. For each game, they invented brand-new rules. And when they got tired of the rules, they changed them.

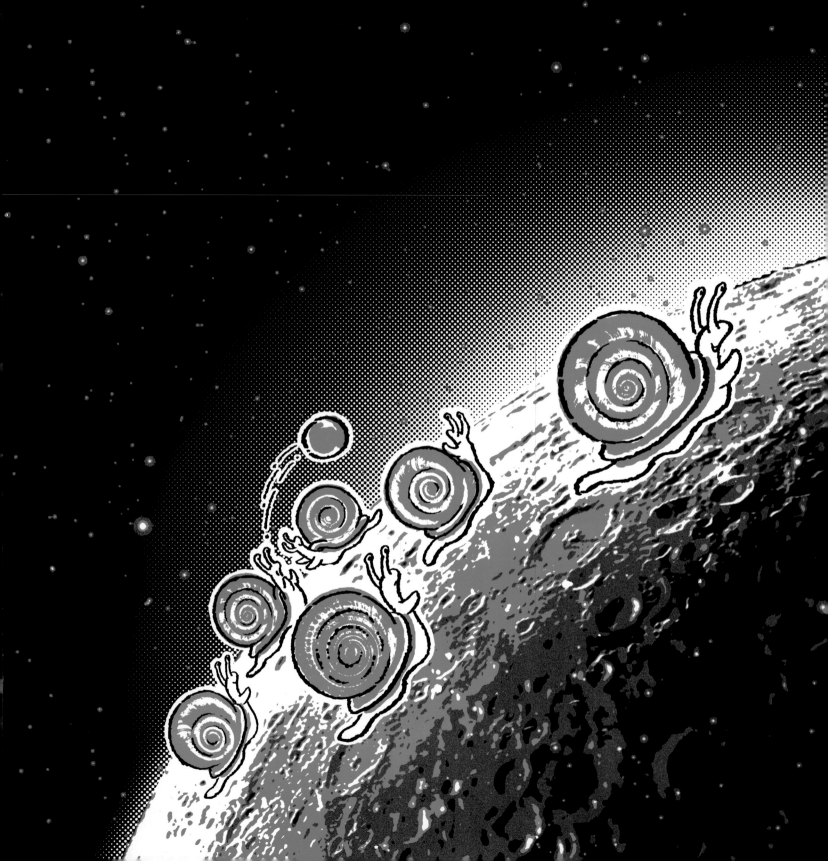

After a while, the moon was only a sliver in the darkness and Willoughby could see his closet door. He waved farewell to his new friend, but the snail was having too much fun to stop for long.

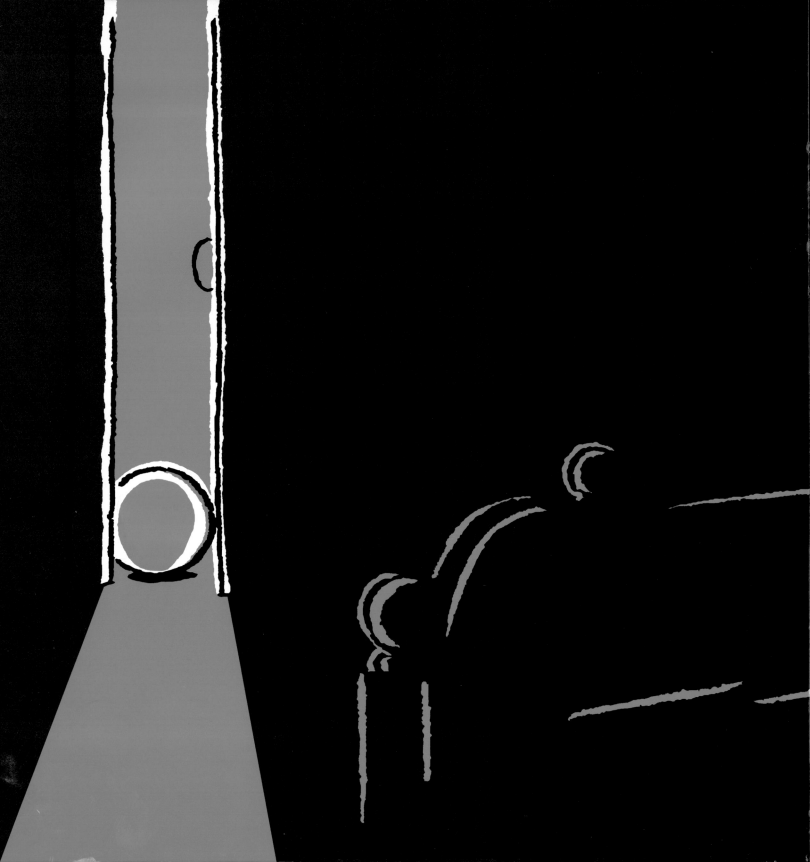

Back in his bedroom, Willoughby could hardly keep his eyes open. And even though the moon wasn't outside his window . . . he knew exactly where it was.

Sleep well.